Undying Romance

CHAPTER ONE

Madison was a very happy chap that always had a warm smile and made me laugh. He thought I was kind of crazy as I told him about my secrets. Unlike Carter, Madison was of short build with dark brown hair and a smile that would melt the heart of any girl.

"I am so glad you are my friend," I said to Madison. "And our friendship shall be filled with laughter and gossip."

"Calm down Anna, your knight in shining armor will come one day and rescue you with open arms!"

"Oh really?" I replied. "Well hurry up and find him!"

Growing up in the countryside was very beautiful. Our tiny little cottage sat at the top of the hill, overlooking the big, bright lights of the city. I liked to sit on the old, wooden summer seat that my dear father had made for me. The seat was made from an old oak tree and it was the most precious thing I had.

My father would go for an evening stroll down into the valley with Skip, his little collie dog. "See you soon Anna!" my father would say. "I shouldn't be gone too long."

Penny was my best friend who also grew up in the countryside, her home was just minutes away from our cottage. Penny and I walked to our little country school every morning which was just a mere ten minutes away from our home. We laughed as we exchanged stories of what we shall do in the forthcoming years.

"Wow Anna, it's a fairytale you want!" Penny exclaimed as she threw her head back laughing.

"I will follow my dreams," I said, "just watch me."

The smell of bacon and eggs on Saturday morning was beautiful. I jumped out of bed and rushed to the breakfast table where my father would be waiting for me.

"Good morning my girl. How did you sleep?" he would say in his very soft voice. "What shall you be doing today Anna?" my father asked.

"Today Penny and I are going to see Mr. Watson to ask him if we can make a swing on the big, old, oak tree.

"You must make sure you do ask the gentleman, Anna," my father said, "after all, the tree belongs to him." I ran to Penny's house, calling her name as I sang merrily. As Penny came out to meet me I told her that my father had gone to see Mr. Watson to ask him about the swing

""Wow," she said, "I hope he says yes!" Grabbing Penny by the hand, I led her to the home of Mr. Watson where my father stood chatting to the gentleman. I was overjoyed when the gentleman agreed to let us have the use of the tree.

"Oh thank you Mr. Watson!" I exclaimed, jumping with excitement.

"But the most important thing right now Anna," my father said sternly, "is that Mr. Watson and I erect the swing and make sure that it is very safe and secure for you!"

Later that afternoon, Penny and I watched as both men made sure the swing they had made was safe and that we enjoyed days of pleasure on it. I couldn't thank the kind, old gentleman enough as I jumped with happiness.

"Ok," Penny said, "you can have the pleasure of using the swing first Anna. After all, it was your idea!" As I sat upon the swing, I felt I had everything. The swing got higher and higher. "This is amazing!" I shouted at the top of my voice. I felt like a bird in my very own world.

I spent all my long, summer days at the swing with Penny. I felt like a bird in my very own world, gathering my thoughts about my future. I kept telling myself that one day I will meet my King, and fly away to a place called paradise.

The higher the swing took me, something wonderful caught my eye. Looking across the valley I could see the sparkling ocean, and there it stood, the most beautiful lighthouse I had ever seen. I felt like it was calling me.

"I would like to go to the lighthouse" I said to my father.

"And one day you will, my child."

Penny and I loved the country life. We planted a tiny little sycamore tree with the help of my dear father and Mr. Watson. "We must visit this tree everyday" I said to Penny.

"And so we shall, Anna!"

"It's my tree!" I said to Penny laughing. "I shall name my tree 'Freedom.'"

"What a beautiful name!" my father exclaimed.

The months and years passed by so quickly, and my school days were coming to an end.

"Have you thought about the type of job you would

like to do when you leave school next year, Anna?"
"I would love to be an author," I said, "and write as many books as I possibly can." From eight years of age, writing became my passion. Sitting beside the old, log fire in the winter evenings, I would get my pen and paper and start to write. My father would be sitting on his rocking chair singing merrily. Beautiful hymns.

"What is your story about Anna?" he asked.

"I am writing a fairytale," I replied, "But a true one, that one day I would like to marry a King and live in a castle."

"Now that sounds very interesting!" my father exclaimed, "but I want you to remember that you will always be my little princess. Always."

When the weather became warmer and the nights got a little brighter, I went down to the lighthouse to write. What beauty surrounded me down there! I would spend many evenings there. As I started to glide my pen across the page, I started to notice the beauty of my words appearing. I would look towards the sky to watch as the seagulls hovered above me. I felt like I was in a different world. My mother passed away when I was very young and my father didn't come to terms with losing his beloved. Nevertheless, my father and I had an amazing bond and in my years of growing up, I did many chores around the cottage while father was at work. I was sitting on my summer seat on a warm summer's evening, looking around at the beauty we had in our countryside. Watching and listening to the birds as they sang so sweetly, landing on the grass and fetching worms to feed their offspring. Suddenly something caught the corner of my eye. A tiny little robin landed on the summer seat just inches away from me! I gazed for a moment at this beautiful, tiny bird then slowly I stretched out my hand towards her and to my amazement; she jumped onto my fingertips. She was so light; yet so very beautiful and content to just sit with me. My father had just returned from his evening stroll.

"How did you do that Anna?"

"Shush, please don't frighten her away!" Then in an instant she flew away. "That was amazing wasn't it?" I said.

"Yes Anna, it sure was! And very touching also may I add" my father said. "Let's go in and have some supper, I have some good news for you!"

"What is it?" I said eagerly.

"Earlier today while I was at work I got chatting to a gentleman who runs a family business! He told me that one of his secretaries is leaving and he was going to advertise her job in the local job column. The job is in the city Anna," my father told me. "And I have told him about you. He said he would like to arrange an interview for you to go and see him!"

"Oh that would be fantastic!" I exclaimed. "I would still be able to write in my spare time. I'm so excited and can't wait to meet him!" I rushed up to tell Penny my good news. "Wow you are a lucky girl!" she said. "I hope I get my job as a dental assistant," Penny added.

"You will, I know you will! But you will be going to live in the city Penny, I won't as you know I love the country, and working in the city is grand, but here is my home."

CHAPTER TWO

Putting on my best skirt and jacket I started to feel the nerves build up inside me. "You'll be just fine!" my father assured me. It seemed as though I had grown up very fast and going to work in the big city was just amazing. I would get to meet lots of people and make new friends. I couldn't wait. As I stood waiting in the hallway facing the reception, I could see the staff sitting at their desks and they all looked so very happy. "Oh father!" I said, "I hope I get the job here. I want to be here so much!"

The atmosphere was very pleasant and the office was very bright. My eyes began to wander around the office and that's when I noticed the vacant desk. *"Oh I hope that desk will be mine!"* I thought to myself. A few moments later, a very tall gentleman walked towards my father and I. "Good morning Sam," the gentleman said as he shook hands with my father.

"And a very good morning to you too Joe," my father replied. "May I introduce you to my daughter, Anna" my father said.

"I'm very pleased to meet you, Sir!" I said, as I shook the gentleman's hand.

"Please, come into my office where we can have a chat," he said with a smile. "Now then, Anna your father has told me so much about you and your love of writing." I felt so much at ease as I answered the very pleasant man. I started to talk about my dreams of working in the city and facing many exciting challenges. I found myself getting carried away, not knowing when to stop. Suddenly I felt my father nudge my arm, I blushed. "Let

Anna continue, Sam," the gentleman said.

"Well it looks like I have just found myself a new secretary. I hope you enjoy working here Anna. And I would like you to call me Joe," my boss said as I thanked him. Joe set my starting date for the second week in July. I couldn't believe what I was hearing. I was so happy. "Let me introduce you to your new work colleagues!"

As I followed Joe into the main office, I noticed my father standing looking at me, so proud of his once tiny, little, girl who was now a young woman. "I would like all of you to meet Anna!" Joe said. "Anna shall be joining us come July." Everyone was so pleasant and greeted me with such happy smiles and after chatting to everyone I knew this was the place for me.

Travelling home in the car with my father, I couldn't stop talking about my job and how proud I would make him. "Anna I am so happy to have such a wonderful daughter. Just go into the city and enjoy your job." Until I passed my driving test, my father would take me to work and collect me to bring me home again. "How was your first day Anna?"

"Oh father, I love it! The people are so friendly. I am going to enjoy my work. I felt like a Queen on her throne when I was sitting at my desk! This job is just what I wanted." Just over a year later I passed my driving test and my father's gift to me was my very own car. Unfortunately this was the last gift he ever gave to me as just over three months later my dear father passed away.

As I was sitting at my desk typing, I overheard a

male voice say "Who is the new girl?" As I lifted my head, I saw a lovely smile upon the guy's face. "This is Anna," Zara said. "Let me introduce you to her." "Madison," Zara said, "this is Anna. Anna, this is Madison."

"It's a pleasure to meet you Anna!" Madison said with a smile as he shook my hand. "You will be seeing a lot of me," he said. "I bring the deliveries into the office twice a week."

"What a really lovely chap," I said to Zara, once Madison had left. "And so very pleasant also." Over the weeks I found myself talking to Madison as if we had known one another for years, telling him about my future, hopes and dreams. On a Monday afternoon as I was standing in my office chatting to Madison, when I noticed the most handsome man I had ever seen walking towards us. My heart skipped a beat. I couldn't take my eyes off him! Madison saw the look on my face and I knew he could read my every thought. "Hi Carter, how are things with you?" Madison asked. Carter's eyes met mine, then, he slowly turned to Madison and replied, "I'm good thanks! Oh by the way, I'm the other delivery guy," Carter said smiling. "So you'll be seeing a lot of me also." Carter was tall, with dark hair and had the most beautiful brown eyes I had ever seen. This guy had just stolen my heart, and from that moment on, my life had changed.

As each day passed, I couldn't wait to see Carter again. I found myself getting carried away with crazy, but beautiful thoughts of Carter and I. Carter drove a high powered motor bike and every time I saw him standing in his soft, leather clothing, my heart would race. Over a week had passed and

Carter still hadn't come into the office. I couldn't wait to see Madison to ask about Carter and tell him about my secret love for this beautiful man. On a Wednesday morning as I was coming back from my coffee break, I could hear Madison talking to Zara. Just as I walked into the office Zara said, "Anna! Madison was just asking for you." It was as if he read my mind when he said, "Carter is off this week, he has gone to a motorbike race. You do like him Anna, don't you?"

"Yes I do," I replied. "Very much. Would you please do me a favor?" I asked Madison.

"Of course I will Anna." I scribbled my extension number onto a post-it note and asked Madison to pass it on to Carter. "This I shall do Anna," he said. "I'll go and find your King." I laughed at his words. "Find my King? Oh please do!"

Every time the phone would ring at my desk, my heart would jump. I just waited for him to call. "Good morning," I said, as I answered the phone. "You are speaking to Anna. How can I help you?"

"Good morning Anna! This is your King calling to wish you a good day at work." I nearly dropped the phone in my excitement. My heart was racing as I tried to control the nerves in my voice. "I saw Madison last night and he asked me to give you a call! Would you like to meet after work and go for a coffee?" Carter asked.

"That would be very nice," I replied.

"I will meet you in the coffee shop around five fifteen."

"Yes Carter, I shall meet you there."

I couldn't wait to see Madison to thank him for finding my King, I laughed to myself. Madison, with his selfless, winning personality had a smile that would melt the heart of many. He would laugh at me every time I mentioned Carter's name. The hours were passing very quickly and it was nearly time to finish my day at the office. I went to the staff room to tidy up my hair and quickly apply my lipstick. *"I hope I can control the nerves in my voice,"* I said to myself. I seated myself down at a table in the coffee shop and moments later there he was, walking towards me. In that instant, my world changed for the better. "Good evening Anna," he said in that sexy, deep voice of his. "Did you have a pleasant day at work?"

"Yes, I did," I replied. "Thank you." As he sat beside me, I could hear every beat of my heart. It was racing like crazy horses in a field. I could smell the leather off his clothing and it drove me wild with desire. I wanted him so much, but knew only time would tell. As we drank our coffee and chatted, I started to feel at ease. Our eyes locked many times and I knew we were both thinking the same thing. Shortly after an hour or so, Carter asked me if I would like to go for a walk in the park. "Yes," I replied. "That would be nice."

"Let's sit under the tree Anna, and just watch the river flow!" As we sat chatting, I began to tell Carter about my life as a country girl and also about which hobbies I enjoyed.

"You are truly an amazing girl, Anna!" I felt my face blush and felt slightly embarrassed. "And you sure do like to talk!" he said.

"Oh Carter," I said, "I am so sorry! I do go on a bit," I muttered in a very quiet voice. Carter placed his hand upon my cheek and as our eyes locked slowly, our lips met. His lips were warm and ever so soft. I felt the desire course throughout my entire body. Our lips locked together for some time and I could feel the love and passion drive me insane. I looked at my watch. "My goodness! It's after 8:00PM. I must start making my way home!" I said to Carter.

"Would you like to go for dinner on Saturday evening?" Carter asked.

"Yes, that would be lovely," I smiled.

"I'll phone you tomorrow and arrange the time."

I couldn't wait to get home and phone Penny. I must tell her my good news! As soon as I got home I phoned Penny to ask her to meet me in the city the next day after work. We arranged to meet at the usual place, which was at the coffee shop.

As Penny and I sat having our coffee I felt myself trying to tell her so much in one breath. "My goodness Anna, take it easy and slow down!" she laughed.

"Ok then," I said. "Come to my cottage on Saturday afternoon and I'll make us lunch, then I can tell you about Carter."

There were never two days the same at the office, but I enjoyed the challenges which I encountered day after day, never knowing what each day was going to be like. But it did not stop me in any way from being my jolly self. I always had that smile, even when life didn't play fair with me. My life to Penny was an open book, as Penny was like a sister to me. We travelled to many beautiful places in the world together and truly, we always had a fantastic time. No matter when I needed Penny she would always be there for me. When I was trying to come to terms with the loss of my parents Penny was always by my side. A true friendship which I shall forever treasure.

"Oh Anna, I am so happy for you and I truly hope this is your dream!"

"Carter is my dream Penny, I know he is."

"My goodness Anna, this is starting to sound like a fairytale already! But when will I get to meet him?" Penny asked.

"In time," I replied. "In time."

CHAPTER THREE

My alarm goes off as usual at 6.30AM and up I get for yet another busy day at the office. Still every thought in my head is of Carter. As I walked down the corridor of my work the first person to greet me would be Zara, and in a very polite voice she would always say, "Good morning Anna. How is your book coming along?" Zara was a very pretty girl with long, red hair and the most beautiful smile. She was a proper lady and everyone loved her. Many times I noticed her look at me with a cheeky smile whenever Carter came in with the deliveries. It was as if she knew we had been dating, but Carter and I wanted this to remain quiet as we wanted to get to know one another first. Over the coming months, Carter and I spent so many wonderful times together and I knew I was falling in love with him. Carter was a very private guy and he liked to keep his work and private life apart and this I respected. Every moment we spent together was blissful and every time I looked into those big brown eyes I melted. I wanted him to make love to me at that very moment, but I knew he had a lot of respect for me and just didn't want to rush things.

Every morning I received a phone call from Carter and in that deep, sexy voice he would say "Good morning my Queen, how are you this morning?"
"My King," I giggled "I am fine thank you."
"I love to hear you voice first thing every morning and last thing every night." Carter said. "Yes darling," I replied "and I feel the same. Let me cook you a meal on Saturday night" I asked.

"That sounds lovely Anna." Carter replied.

Carter had not been to the cottage as yet, so come Saturday he shall see how beautiful the countryside looks and also, my little cottage. The following day as I sat at my desk in work, all I could think about was how romantic Saturday night was going to be. I had everything planned to perfection. Then on Friday afternoon sitting at my desk, my telephone rang.

"Good afternoon Anna."

"Hi Carter," I said "how are you?"

"Oh Anna! I am so sorry but I have to cancel Saturday night." he said.

My heart sank and I didn't know what to say.

"Is everything alright, Carter?" I asked.

"You are a beautiful girl Anna, but I'm afraid I can't give you the love you truly deserve." My eyes began to fill up with tears and in a very low voice I said, "Oh Carter, please don't say that."

"Anna, I am so sorry this is the hardest thing I have had to do and the last thing I want to do is hurt you. Please let us remain friends," he said "I promise you Anna, you are never to far from my mind but..."

"Stop," I said "just leave me alone. How can you do this to me?"

I managed to fight back the tears until I got home that evening. I lay awake most of the night, pondering the harsh words Carter had spoken on the phone in the previous hours. We got on so well and I just couldn't understand why he would do this to me. I cried myself to sleep that night but also prayed I would awake to find this was all just a bad dream. I had fallen in love with Carter, and I just couldn't let him go. I needed a reason as to why he wanted to end what we had.

I pottered about the cottage all weekend trying to keep myself and my mind busy, but to no avail, as every thought in my head was about the man I loved and wanted. My weekend felt like a lifetime and I couldn't wait until I got back to work on Monday morning. I had to pull myself together as I couldn't possibly let my work colleagues see me in such a mess. Every time the phone rang at my desk my heart jumped "I only wish he would call me," I said to myself "I want to know what went wrong between us."

Looking at the clock in work, I couldn't believe the time, it was home time already, but I just didn't want to go home. "Bye everyone!" I heard Zara say. "Bye Zara. See you tomorrow." I said.

As I entered through the front door of my cottage, I ran and threw myself on top of my bed crying buckets of tears and calling Carter's name.
"Why did you do this to me?!" I shouted "Why?!"
I fell into a sleep and awoke shortly after 2am. I got changed into my nightwear and set my alarm for 6am.
"*Pull yourself together Anna*," I said to myself "*you have to be strong*". My alarm goes off at 6am and I go to make myself a strong cup of coffee before I get my morning shower. I tried not to think too much of Carter but this was so very hard to do.

Zara had made me a coffee and placed it on my desk. "Oh thank you, Zara" I said. "Please excuse me but I must get these invoices completed."

"Anna are you alright? You haven't been yourself these past couple of days."

"Yes Zara I'm fine. I just have a bit of a headache I will be grand."

Shortly before lunchtime I answered my phone and to my amazement, it was Carter!

"Anna," he said "please forgive me I feel like such a silly fool!" I want to meet you after work today if that is alright with you? Please meet me Anna I need to talk to you."

"Yes I will meet you," I replied "but you can't hurt me anymore Carter, this is so unfair on me." Let's meet in the park," I said "it's such a nice evening."

As I sat in the park waiting for him, everything was going through my head but inside, I felt so happy he was coming to meet me. Then seconds later I heard the sound of his motorbike he drove up to where I was sitting and removed his helmet. My heart skipped a beat. "Hi Anna" he said "how are you?"

"I am fine. A little tired, but fine thank you."

He sat down beside me on the summer seat, his eyes fixed firmly on mine and before I knew it we had both thrown our arms around one and other were kissing passionately. Our lips were locked and we both couldn't stop as the urge of wanting each other became stronger. Chills were racing through my entire body, I didn't want this moment to ever end. As we kissed, I moaned with uncontrollable urge, "Oh Carter, I need you."

I said as his warm lips moved slowly down my neck. I just couldn't stop the words from rolling off my lips. Carter lifted me and sat me upon his knee.

"I truly missed you, Anna." he said. "Why did you leave me Carter?" I said in a low, sad voice.

He placed his fingertips upon my lips and said "Please Anna, don't say anymore. I must say how stupid I was to even do such a thing to someone so precious to me. How would you like to go away for a night, Anna?" he said.

"Yes I would like very much."

"I know the perfect place and I know you will enjoy it immensely. Let me walk you to your car Anna and I shall phone you later tonight just to make sure you got home safe."

I couldn't wait until I got home, just to hear the sound of his strong, sexy voice again. I got myself tucked up in my bed and just waited for his call.

"Hello my Queen. I take it you got home safe?"

"Yes darling, I did."

"I tried to resist you Anna, but I failed and I am glad I did because you are the most wonderful girl I have ever known. Let me call you tomorrow and arrange that special evening away for us" he said. "Thank you for being there this evening Anna."

"I will always be here for you, Carter" I replied.

I lay awake for some time, just thinking about our night away together and how special it was going to be. *"Am I just starting to live my fairytale?"* I thought to myself. Well I knew this man had won my heart, my mind and my body and deep inside, I knew I had found my soul mate.

Just as I was getting ready to leave for work my phone rang. "Good morning my Queen, the taste of your lips, which lingered with me throughout the night, the smell of your beautiful perfume and even the touch of your soft skin is driving me wild with lust for you. My Queen I must tell you that I find you behind every door in my mind as you are always there."

"I must say you have a beautiful way with words, Carter."

"Not as beautiful as you have my queen. Today I shall make arrangements for our night away and call you later with the date."

"That's good," I said " I look forward to it."

I called Penny after work and told her that Carter and I are going away for a night.

"Oh Anna I am so glad and I hope it goes well for you both and don't forget to call me and let me know how it goes!"

"I sure will," I said to Penny "I sure will."

Just as I was getting into bed that evening, Carter phoned me.

"Hello my Queen, I have booked us a room at a beautiful hotel. Does next Saturday suit you?"

"Of course it does." I replied and I was sure he heard the excitement in my voice. I just couldn't wait to be alone with Carter again.

Walking into the office on Monday morning as usual I was greeted with that bubbly smile from Zara.

"Good morning Anna. You have that look off love written all over your face."

"Oh Zara stop it!" I said "Please don't have me blushing and then the rest of the guys will start to ask questions."

"I think I know your secret Anna." Zara said with a cheeky wink.

"Now then, I have lots of work to do," I blurted out,

"so I must get dash."

"Alright then Anna, but you will tell me all about it one day." Zara whispered and she left me to my work.

My days in work that week were very busy and thank goodness Friday was drawing to a close. Just as I was clearing up my last few invoices to be put on file, I heard that happy voice say "Hi Anna what has been happening?" I jumped up from my seat and gave Madison a big hug.

"Have I got news for you!" I said as I giggled.

"What have you done to Carter?" Madison said with a smile. "You have blown that guy's mind Anna, he's in love!"

"Really?" I said "How can you tell?"

"Oh I can tell, Anna! I think he is your perfect king, may I add!" Madison laughed as I told him that I called Carter my King and Carter called me his Queen.

"He does have another pet name for me," I said "but I shall keep it to myself at the moment."

"I am so happy for you both Anna! Carter is a great guy and let me say he has found himself an amazing woman."

"We will meet up for a chat next week" I promised.

"Well I hope you both have a wonderful time on your evening away!"

"See you next week Madison! I hope you have a nice weekend as well."

I couldn't even eat my dinner when I got home from work because I was bursting with happiness about our evening away. I had a hot, relaxing bath and made myself a hot chocolate and just as I got settled into bed, Carter called me.

"I shall pick you up tomorrow Anna around 2pm." he said.

I gave Carter my address and the directions to my cottage. I couldn't wait for him to come and see my little home and the beauty and love which it held.

Finally the day arrives and shortly after breakfast, I start to pack my overnight bag. I packed my beautiful white knee length dress it was made of pure cotton and around the bottom where little tiny butterflies made from diamonds. I decided that I would roll my hair up and tie a white cotton band around it when I wore my dress. I couldn't wait to see Carters face, I wanted to look real pretty for him.

Shortly before 2pm Carter arrived at the cottage. As I opened the door to greet him, I saw him standing looking around.

"What a beautiful place Anna!" he said "This place is absolutely wonderful! Now I know why you love the country life so much. It's breathtakingly beautiful."

"Come inside and let me show you my little castle." I said with a smile.

As we entered into the cottage I watched as Carter looked around.

"You sure do have a beautiful home, Anna. I can tell that is a place filled with love and beauty."

"Thank you" I beamed. "Let me cook dinner for us next week and then I will take you down into the valley and show you where my friend Penny and I used to play."

"Now that sounds good! I look forward to it."

As we drove into the city, I noticed we were driving

towards the most beautiful hotel I had ever seen.

"My goodness Carter, this place is like a castle!" I said.

"Yes my Queen. I want nothing but the best for you." he replied with a soft smile.

I felt my eyes fill up with tears but had to very quickly pull myself together.

"Wait until I tell Penny about this... wow she will not believe it" I said to myself.

Carter got our bags from the car as I stood looking around me. I had never in my wildest dreams imagined I would be staying in a place so beautiful. As we walked up to the reception desk we were greeted by a very lovely lady who introduced herself to Carter and I. Her name was Katie. We both shook hands with her as she wished us a pleasant stay.

"Leo will show you to your room." Katie said "Give me a moment and I'll call him. If you should need anything please just phone down to reception, we are here to help." Seconds later a young man appeared. He seemed somewhat shy and had a very soft voice.

"Good afternoon Sir." he said to Carter. "I am Leo, the porter. Let me show you both to your room." Leo opened our bedroom door and carried in our overnight bags and set them down on the floor beside the bed. "I hope you both have a pleasant stay."

"Thank you Leo. I am sure we will." I replied.

Our bedroom was outstanding. The massive four post bed looked like something from a fairytale. The carpet was deep red and the walls were cream.

"This place is just heavenly, Carter." I said.

I started to unpack my bag but I didn't want Carter to see what I had chosen to wear that evening so quickly, I slipped it into the wardrobe hoping he wouldn't see it. We both then went down to look around the rest of the hotel and what a breathtaking place it was.

"Oh my goodness! This place is massive!" I gasped as I looked around at the many function rooms but the one that caught my eye was the ballroom.

"Let's go and have a drink, Anna." Carter said, as he steered me towards the bar area. Carter ordered the drinks and I excused myself to go to the ladies.

"I hope you like your room, Anna." Katie said as I was returning from the ladies room. "Yes thank you, it's beautiful." I said.

"Remember, Anna, if you need anything at all just call me."

"Actually Katie, there is just one thing I would love you to do for me but only if it's possible."

"Anna whatever it is I would only be too happy to help."

"Would you be able to come up to our room later and help me get ready for dinner, please? I would like your opinion on what I have chosen to wear."

"Of course. No problem Anna! Just phone down and I will get Leo to cover the desk." "Oh thank you Katie, you are a star!"

When I arrived at the table where Carter was sitting he smiled and said "I see you and Katie have become friends already."

I laughed as I said "Yes. Katie will be coming to the room later to help me with my hair. Is that alright with you?"

"My Queen, I shall make myself scarce." he said

laughing. "Tell you what... while you are in the bathroom having your shower I will get myself ready and go down to the bar and have a drink. I'll ask Katie to come up to you once I get downstairs. Would that be ok?"

"Perfect" I thought "Yes that would be grand Carter but only if you don't mind."

CHAPTER FOUR

Slipping into my dress that evening I noticed Katie was stood staring at me.

"Oh Anna you already look so very beautiful! she exclaimed. As Katie zipped up the back of my dress she said "Carter is a very lucky man. You will blow him away when he sets eyes on you."

As I stood looking at myself in the long mirror I asked Katie to help me with my chain. I explained to her that my friend Penny bought me this chain when I passed my driving test, "it means so much to me" I told her as she put it on me.

"That's you ready now Anna. Your King will be here in a few minutes. Have a wonderful evening and I'll see you both later." As I stood looking at myself in the mirror the door opened and there he stood.

He looked even more handsome than usual. We stood what seemed like a lifetime staring at each other. He was wearing a beautiful grey suit, white shirt and navy tie. My mind was racing and I wanted him that very instant.

"Anna, my Queen, you look absolutely beautiful, you're driving me wild."

"You are the most handsome man I have ever set eyes on and from this moment, you are all I want. You, Carter, are my perfect dream."

"I can't take my eyes off you." he said as he walked slowly towards me. He took me in his arms and kissed me. Let's go and have dinner now, we have got all evening to make plans! *"Make plans?"* I thought. *"what plans?"*

On our arrival at the restaurant Leo was standing

by to show us to our table.

"Good evening." he said with a cute smile "You look lovely" he said.

"Thank you" I replied blushing.

We sat down at our table that overlooked the beautiful, big lawn, the candle in the centre of the table was red and sat in a tiny glass bowl.

"This is a wonderful place." I said to Carter. "Everything is just perfect, the carpet was red and made the cream walls look amazing. The glass chandelier hanging from the ceiling and the art on the walls is just perfect."

"You make it complete Anna. I only want the best for you."

"You have really gone to a lot of trouble doing this," I said, "you make me feel..." I trailed off as I couldn't find the words I wanted to say.

"Don't say anything my Queen. Let' enjoy every minute we have." he said as we smiled warmly at each other.

Leo arrived at our table with a bottle of champagne. "Thank you, Leo" we both said as he poured it into the glasses. Our meal arrived and I couldn't eat much as I was brimming over with terrible excitement. I caught Leo a few times from the corner of my eye watching me. I excused myself from the table to go to the ladies room,

"I won't be long" I said "just a few moments."

I wanted to apply my lipstick and perfume and take a few deep breaths. This was truly an amazing evening. Walking back to the table I heard the small voice say,

"Carter is one lucky man." I gave a tiny shy smile, it was Leo.

After our meal we remained at the table chatting. We finished the rest of the bottle of champagne and by this time we were both giggling and while looking into one another's eyes. Our eyes and bodies said it all.

"Lets go out and take a stroll through the garden, I would love to see its beauty." I said. We held hands as we left the restaurant, saying good evening to Leo.

"This place sure is something" I gushed.

We walked for about half an hour through the garden, it was just so peaceful.

"Just listen to the birds," I said, "they are singing so sweetly and they seem so happy and carefree."

Walking through the garden that led us back to the hotel we saw Katie.

"Katie, Anna and I would like to thank you immensely for everything you did for us this evening" Carter said.

"It was an absolute pleasure" Katie replied. "I wish you both a very enjoyable evening and maybe we'll meet again sometime. Well that's me off for a few days now" she said, "enjoy your time off and relax."

We arrived back to the room, Carter opened the door and said "after you."

"Would you like a coffee?" he asked, "yes, thank you" I said."

I kicked off my shoes and sat on top of the bed.

"This bed is massive," I laughed "I would get lost in it very easily."

Carter walked over to the wardrobe to hang up his jacket, he removed his tie and opened the first two buttons of his shirt. I wanted to pull him close to me as I saw his chest exposed. I stood up and walked over to him.

"I want to tell you how happy I am and that this is the best night of my life."

He took me in his arms and kissed me. He pulled the zip at the back of my dress down and my dress fell to the floor. I opened every button on his shirt, this guy had the perfect body. The smell of his aftershave blew me away with lust. I stepped out of my dress and then still kissing me he undid my bra. While he was kissing and caressing every part of me I said "please Carter take me now, this is our moment."

He lifted me up and lay me down so gently on the bed. I slipped off my white satin, skimpy pants.

"Oh Anna! You are just perfect in every way."

I watched as he removed his trousers, it was time to enter into our very own heaven.

We were both naked and as we kissed and touched every part of each other's naked bodies. The passion was over powering. As he gently kissed my inner thighs he sent the blood racing through my body and then our bodies became one!

"I have finally reached heaven" he said as we made love.

I felt every inch of him as he penetrated my womanhood and with every bit of strength I had I held onto him so tightly not wanting to let go. Our love making was unbelievable, I felt the adrenalin rush through my body at the same as time I cried out with pleasure.

"I love you Carter and want you to be mine forever." I whispered in his ear.

Holding my head he placed his lips upon mine, this time even harder than ever before. Then after what seemed like a lifetime, I looked into his eyes and saw his immense pleasure. His strong body started to move even faster and as he said "Anna I love you."

We both reached that moment that we had been waiting for. Never in my wildest dreams did I think it was going to be so beautiful. We lay there holding each other for some time and placing a gentle kiss on my lips he said to me,

"I never want my Queen to stop loving me."

"I never will," I replied, "I have found my King and together we will live our dream." Carter and I drifted off to sleep still holding each other. I woke up to find him sitting on the chair by the window in our room.

"Are you alright Carter?" I asked.

"Yes my Queen, I am, I just wanted to sit here and watch you as you slept. You looked so very peaceful, just like Sleeping Beauty."

"Come back to bed," I said "it is only 5.30am."

"I keep thinking this is a dream" he said with a smile. "I am going to go and have a shower, I will be back in about ten minutes." he said.

"I'll make some coffee."

As I listened to the shower running I just could not resist taking a peek so I opened the bathroom door and there he stood the water was cascading down his big strong body. He noticed me standing in the doorway. As I stood there watching him he stretched out his hand and, letting my bathrobe fall to the floor, I stepped into the shower to join him. As the water ran down our naked bodies we held on to each other so tightly kissing and moaning with uncontrollable pleasure we made love again.

"Oh Anna, my Queen, I love you and I want you to promise me that you won't ever leave me."

As we both returned to the bedroom we lay on top of the bed talking about what we both would like to do in the future and also talked about places where we both would like to visit during the holiday season. Later that day we checked out of the hotel around 3pm and as we drove back to my cottage I could not stop thinking about our time together. It was magical. Carter got my bag from the car and said

"I won't come in because I want to get back and see how my father is doing but I will call you tonight at the usual time 10pm." he smiled.

I decided to phone Penny to let her know I was home and also to tell her I had an amazing time.

"Oh Penny! I am in love and everything was just so perfect!"

"You sure are one lucky girl!" Penny said "If you are not doing anything tomorrow after work I will come to the cottage for tea and you can tell me all about it."

"I'll see you around 6.30 then."

I made myself a hot chocolate and got myself tucked up in bed waiting on Carter to phone me. At 10pm on the dot my telephone rang. I longed to hear that strong voice again, it drove me insane with want for him.

"Good evening my Queen. Let me first of all say thank you for such a wonderful time, I can't stop thinking about you. Every second you are constantly on my mind."

"Oh Carter, I feel the same! I truly enjoyed myself so much."

"I have found my perfect Queen" he said. I felt my heart racing as he said those words did he truly mean this?

"Why don't you come down to the cottage next Friday after work?" I asked Carter "We could spend the weekend together."

"Yes, I would really like that and you can take me to that waterfall you always tell me about and let me see the rest of the beauty down in the countryside."

I was so excited when I put the phone down after our goodnight wishes. I was going to make our weekend so unforgettable.

Driving on my way to work the following morning as usual thinking of Carter and saying to myself *"I hope Madison calls into the office today. I have so much to tell him."*

"Well, good morning everyone" I said as I arrived at the office. As usual, Zara winked and said "Good morning Anna. Have you anything you wish to tell me?"

I smiled and said "Zara, one day I'll tell you my story but until then I am afraid you'll have to be in suspense for a little longer."

"Well hello Anna!" a jolly voice gushed from behind.

I didn't even have to look up as I knew that jolly voice was Madison! Getting up from my desk I gave him a big hug and said "Oh I am so glad to see you! I have lots of news for you. Have you time for a coffee?" I asked Madison.

"Of course I do" he laughed, "Well lets go outside and you can tell me how your King is." I couldn't stop laughing at him.

"You make me laugh the way you always say my 'King'" I said with a chuckle.

I began to tell Madison as much as I could, "I wish I had all day Madison. I have lots of great news for you. But anyway, I am so madly in love with Carter and I am very happy."

"Yes Anna I can see that," he said with a cheeky smile, "it is written all over your face and to be honest, I know Carter is in love with you too and I really am happy for you both. You seem like the perfect couple and I truly mean that."

"I feel like I am living in a fairytale." I said.

"You are Anna but a true one. Please tell Carter I said hi."

"Of course I will."

Carter had left his delivery job with our company several weeks ago so Madison didn't get to see him much. His new job meant he would have to travel down south on a daily basis but Carter enjoyed this and I was very happy for him. At least we had nearly every weekend together and the odd evening during the week and no matter what he always made the time for me.

I was really looking forward to seeing Penny after work so I stopped off at the fish shop and got us a nice piece of fish for tea. After I set the table and put some logs on the fire it was nearly time for my best friend to arrive.

As soon as I heard Penny's car I ran to the door to meet her and there she was walking up the driveway with a smile from ear to ear.

"Let's eat first and then I'll tell you what a great time I am having with my King." Penny roared laughing.

"King?! You call him your King?! Oh Anna, you are crazy aren't you?"

"Stop it Penny!" I said as I blushed, but Penny just continued to laugh.

"Oh never mind then." I said with a smile.

As I told her of my love for Carter she sat looking at me with tears in her eyes, but tears of happiness for Carter and I.

"You always said you wanted to live a fairytale Anna. Listening to this, I think you will get all your heart desires."

My little cottage was just perfect but after my father passed away, I had added a few modern touches to it and changed the colour of the decor. I did not in any way want to erase the beautiful memories that my home held. We went on to chat about the days when we were growing up and what wonderful memories we did recall.

"You know Anna, I can still feel the love and warmth here just like old times." Penny was an only child just like myself. We both talked about our parents and remembered that every Sunday morning we all attended our little country church that was down in the valley. What beautiful memories Anna she said as a tear fell from her eye..

I love working in the city I said to Penny, but my home shall always be in the country. I just love the beautiful, peaceful surroundings. "Anna have you met Carters family yet?" asked Penny. "No I haven't Penny, but I soon will." I am happy with the way things are but I will meet them in time. Carter lives with his father and whenever the time is right no doubt Carter shall introduce us." Carter was in a relationship for a few years before we met, but things just didn't work out so they both decided to end it. He doesn't talk much of his past but I am happy with that. "You see Penny, all that matters now is Carter and I." Well Anna I truly hope so and hope that you don't get hurt. You are in love with this guy and I can surely see that.

CHAPTER FIVE

I couldn't wait until the weekend as Carter was coming to stay for a couple of days. We shall go down into the valley and I would like to show him the big old tree where Penny and I made our first swing. I heard Carters car pull up on Friday evening. *"Why am I getting so nervous?"* I asked myself. I had to stop this and compose myself, this is going to be a very special and romantic weekend for us both. As I went outside to meet Carter, I just stood looking at him. *"What an amazing, handsome guy."* I thought to myself. "May I say how beautiful you look, my Queen, and I am a very lucky man". "Oh Carter," I blushed, "and I am a very lucky lady". Let me put your overnight bag in the bedroom and we shall have dinner. Every time I looked at Carter my heart would race with excitement.

As I was just adding the finishing touches to our meal, I felt Carter's hands around my waist, and then he began to kiss my neck. I turned around and gently kissed him. "We must eat I said" "Sorry Anna every time I see you I just want to hold you and never let you go. You are an amazing cook Anna," he said smiling. "I thoroughly enjoyed that meal, let me make us a coffee and clear the table" said Carter. We both went outside and sat for a short while. "This is the life Anna, what a beautiful place, so very blissful and also so full of love, now I can see why you would not want to live in the city." "Why don't we go inside," I said, "and I shall put on some music and we can have a glass of wine."

I put some logs on the fire and lit some candles, the place was all lovely and romantic and then Carter and I snuggled up on the couch. "I can't wait to go down to the village tomorrow," said Carter, "and I am also looking forward to seeing the Light House and not to mention the beautiful waterfall." Carter and I made love in front of the fire that evening. The flames from the fire and the flickering of the candle light made everything just as romantic as I had hoped it would ever be. "I am crazy about you Anna" he said as he kissed every part of my body from head to toe. The passion was priceless in our love making and as our bodies became one, I cried aloud with uncontrollable pleasure. "Please don't ever leave me Anna, you are my world and all I live for." A short while after our love making, Carter and I retired to bed.

I awoke to hear Carter singing in the kitchen, making us breakfast. I walked into the kitchen and I just stood there at the door way watching him. Carter was singing the song "Always" by Bon Jovi. I felt a tear fall from my eye just as he turned to set the coffee on the table. I walked towards him and placed a long lingering kiss upon his lips. "Did you sleep well?" I asked Carter. "Yes my queen, I did. I got up around seven thirty and had a shower and I wanted to surprise you with Breakfast. I hope you don't mind? My cooking may not be as good as yours, but I am sure it will get better in time" he laughed. I could smell something burning... "OH NO!" Carter said, the bacon was burnt to a crisp. "You see... I am all fingers and thumbs Anna when I try to do things." "Don't worry, but you do need some lessons in cooking. You just had the oven too high, let me finish making breakfast." I giggled.

Around lunch time I made us some sandwiches and a flask of hot soup, packed a rug into the picnic basket and off we went, hand in hand. "First of all lets go to the waterfall" I said. I could see the excitement in Carter's face as we arrived. "Now Anna, this is absolutely beautiful." Standing in amazement yet again and lost in his very own world, just taking in the beauty left him speechless. "Let us just sit here, Carter" as I laid the blanket at the side of the fall. I started to tell Carter all about my happy childhood years and how this was the place that Penny and I would have come to visit and bring our very own picnic. As usual I got carried away chatting then Carter would lean over and place a kiss upon my lips. "I adore you Anna, I truly do and you never cease to amaze me." Carter held me so tightly in his strong arms and kissing me passionately, I felt like I was in heaven. "I am never going to let you go Anna," he whispered in my ear. My heart began to race as it always had done when he held me in that warm embrace. We both lay for what seemed like hour just listening to the sound of the birds singing and watching the water flowing. "Carter," I said, "I never want us to end." He placed his fingertips upon my lips and softly said "My Queen, it won't I promise you".

"We should go to the lighthouse tomorrow" I said. "On our way back to the cottage I shall take you to see the big old tree where Penny and I made our swing when we were very young." Carter and I were like two children as we held hands and ran through the valley, both out of breath with excitement. "This is the tree I said" as I ran towards it. I felt my mind drifting back once again to my youth and smiled. I watched Carter, as he carved our names onto the tree. "That is just perfect," he said as he stood beside me, "let me see our names" I said as I swung around the beautiful, old tree. "Just like my love for you my Queen, that will never fade."

We both arrived back to the cottage and Carter excused himself to the bathroom. "Would you like a cold drink?" I asked. "Yes Anna, that would be nice, it would most certainly cool us down after all that running," he laughed! As I took the water from the fridge I felt Carters hands as he placed them upon my shoulders, and at that moment I gently turned around to him and kissed him so gently. Carter lifted me up and carried me into the bedroom. As he placed me on the bed, our eyes locked upon one another for a time than seemed like forever.

As he kissed and caressed my entire body, we both started to undress each other and within moments, our bodies became one. The love making was heavenly and the passion was overwhelming, as always for us both. Carter always held me so tight, close to his chest after we made love. "Anna, you are my world." He said to which I replied, "you are mine, My King." We just lay there, talking about anything and everything, but most of all, the love we had for each other.

CHAPTER SIX

Sitting at breakfast the following morning, Penny called me. "Good morning, Anna! I was just thinking... if you are free today, would you like to go a stroll down to the lighthouse?" she said. I replied saying "Carter is with me, but I would be happy if you would like to come for some tea this evening and let me introduce you both?" "So I get to meet the one and only *Carte?*" Penny giggled. "Of course you do, I shall see you around 4pm then" I said to Penny.

"I hope you don't mind if Penny joins us for tea today?" I asked Carter. "That will be nice, I hope she likes me, after all, she is your best friend and wants only the best for you." Carter said sweetly. As Carter and I were walking towards the lighthouse, we stopped and paused for a few minutes. "My god, this place is absolutely beautiful, Anna" Carter said as he gazed into the vast surrounding of countryside. "I love to come down here" I said. "Many times I would bring my pens and book and sit at the lighthouse for hours, just writing."
"So many times you have told me about the sheer beauty here" Carter said, "and now I can see it for myself. I can see why you would never want to leave here, I shall be coming here more often."
"Yes, it is my home and I don't think I could ever leave, in fact, I know I couldn't." I said.

Carter was in the bathroom when Penny arrived. Where is this handsome guy then?" She whispered.

"Oh Penny! Please don't start me laughing, you will see him in just a moment." I laughed.

"Penny," I said, "this is Carter." As he stretched his hand out to say hello, Penny couldn't take her eyes off him. I watched as Carter blushed and said "I am very pleased to meet you, Penny. Anna has told me so much about you."
Penny laughed and said "well I hope it has all been good!"

Penny didn't stay too long, we all had tea and a good old chat. Penny then followed me into the kitchen as I was putting the plates away and burst out saying "my goodness, Anna! He sure is one good looking guy and he's sure crazy about you. Anna, you are living that fairytale after all." "But then, you're very pretty, Anna." "I am only 5foot, Penny," I said, "Carter is 6foot." Anna laughed, amused. "you make a wonderful couple, anyone can see that!"
"Thank you for tea, it was very nice and it was a pleasure to finally meet you, Carter." Penny said with a sweet smile. "And you, Penny." Said Carter.

CHAPTER SEVEN

Sitting at my desk in work, typing up all my invoices, I heard Zara call my name. As I looked across the room to her desk, she gave me a cheeky little nod and wink. I then noticed what she was trying to tell me, without making it obvious. As I looked towards the door, I saw my good friend, Madison, standing there with another guy. "Hi Anna." He said, "this is Connor, Connor will be working with me now." Madison told Connor of our friendship and also explained how I was Carter's girlfriend. "It is a pleasure to meet you," he said. "and you also, Connor!" I said through a smile.

Zara couldn't take her eyes off Connor. After they had left the office, Zara said "that guy is something, and I sure will be having a coffee with him!" Joe, our boss, arrived into the office shortly after lunchtime. He told us that he was taking a couple of months off as he had just bought a new house and had a lot of renovations to carry out, to get it into shape. "Anna, how would you like to take charge while I'm away?" he said.
I couldn't believe what I was hearing, but I said confidently "I would love that, but Zara has been here a lot longer than I have and to be honest, I would say she would be the perfect person for the position. However, thank you ever so much for the offer, I am deeply touched that you considered me first." Zara was over the moon and agreed to take the role until Joe returned.

I then said to the guys in the office, "why don't we go for a nice meal one evening and celebrate Zara's new post?" To which I received a positive response, of course. We all met at 8.30pm the following day in the restaurant and had a beautiful meal, a few glasses of wine, and a lot of laughs. Zara was very excited about taking on this new role and was excited to be the boss for the next few months.

"Now then," she said to me "I will be seeing a lot of Connor and maybe get to know him a bit better."

"Oh Zara, you do like him, don't you?" I said. Zara smiled, and said "I sure do."

I arrived home shortly after 11pm. The first thing I did after getting myself tucked up in bed was to phone Carter. "Did my Queen have a nice evening?" He asked.

"Yes, My King I did but every thought in my head was of you" I said.

Carter stayed with me nearly every weekend at the cottage and everything seemed so perfect when we were together. "Go My Queen and get some sleep, I shall call you tomorrow around lunchtime."

CHAPTER EIGHT

The next morning, Zara was in the kitchen making everyone the morning coffee. She was already starting to enjoy her new role as our boss and generally being her jolly self. Just as she was coming from the kitchen, with the tray of cups, I saw her blush. As I looked towards the door I noticed Madison and Connor. I gave her a smile and said "let me take that tray before you drop it."

"Hi guys," she said to Madison and Connor "would you both like to join us for a coffee?"

"Now that sounds like a good idea." Connor replied and then I caught him staring at her. I was certain at that very moment, he really did like Zara. They got chatting and I could see how happy she was and I could tell there was definitely going to be a serious romance between the two of them. I couldn't wait until Carter arrived to spend the weekend, he said he had something to ask me.

I got into bed early that evening as I was pretty tired and wanted an early night. Carter and I had planned an evening out for a meal in the little country inn. So the next day we were out for our meal and Carter asked "Would you like to go to Paris Anna?" going to Paris had always been one of my dreams and so, overwhelmed I replied "Oh yes, My King, that would be amazing, I would love it, but when would we be going?" "Hopefully in the next few weeks" he replied, with that sexy smile. "I shall mention it to Zara on Monday morning, but it shouldn't be a problem and I could take a week's holiday." I said. "Anna, My Queen I promise I will make every dream you have wished for come true!"

"Paris?!" Zara said. "My goodness, you sure can have a week off, after all you will be making big plans I take it when you come back." "He might not be asking me to be his wife," I said "but I hope he does." I said excitedly. "I am so happy for you both, you are just the perfect couple." Anna exclaimed. "I am a very lucky girl Zara." I said. "Yes, and Carter is a very lucky man!" Zara replied. "If I tell you something, Anna, promise you won't laugh?" Zara said, somewhat embarrassed. "You can tell me anything, Zara and what makes you think I will laugh?" I replied, intrigued.

"I really fancy Connor and I can't stop thinking about him."

"Listen, I say if you want something that much, you go and follow your dream. Ask him out for dinner or even go after work with him for coffee? Personally, I think he likes you too" I replied. "The way he looks at you when he comes into the office..." "Really Anna?" Zara erupted as I was mid-sentence. "Are you being serious Anna?"

"Trust me Zara, he likes you...a lot. I can tell."

"The excitement is really building up inside me about our trip to Paris, I am going to see all the beautiful sights I thought I would only ever dream of!" Right then Zara said "I am going to ask Connor does he want to go out for a meal sometime." Knowing Zara clearly was in a world of her own and not caring what I was saying, I replied "Go girl, just pick up the courage and ask him. You know something Zara, if you start going out with Connor, Madison will think we are crazy. I get Carter and you get Connor, both guys are and were his work colleagues." I said, laughing. "Oh Anna, I don't care, I must get to date this guy!" Zara said.

Zara never stopped talking about Connor and was just waiting on her opportunity to ask him. "well," I said, "you don't have to wait much longer, his van has just pulled up outside." I looked at Zara's face, it was purple. "Calm down," I said "just pull yourself together and go for it."

As Madison and Connor walked into the office, I saw Connor glare search the room for Zara. He walked over to her and gave her some invoice to sign. Her hands were trembling and Connor noticed this. Madison smiled at me and said "Connor really likes Zara." "Well," I replied "I think Zara feels the same way about Connor."

"Do you think he will ask her out?" I asked to Madison.

"Yes, he will, it's only a matter of time. My goodness, Anna, I feel like a matchmaker." He laughed. "Thank goodness you and Zara are the only two females here, I couldn't cope with losing two buddies. Only joking Anna, I hope it works out for them. I hear you and Carter are off to Paris? One thing is for sure, you will both be happy as you were definitely made for each other."

"Bye Zara!" I heard Connor say and when I looked across the office I could see the biggest smile on her face. She winked and said "He asked me out!"

We both went into the kitchen, I wanted to hear how he asked her about a date.

"Anna, I'm still shaking." She said. "I was just about to ask him, but he asked me if I was free some evening and if I would like to go for a meal. I didn't even hesitate, Anna, I immediately said yes!

So we are going out Saturday night."
"Good girl," I said "I am so happy for you."

"Our days at the office seemed to go in very quickly, how time flies" I said. "Yes, it won't be very long until Christmas and in just over a week, you and your beloved will be off to Paris!" Zara said.

I invited Zara down to the cottage for dinner and a chat. "I would like that" she said. "You could bring your pjs and we could have a good old chat and a glass of wine" I added.

"Right then, I could come on Friday if that suits?" Zara asked.

"Of course it does, I won't be seeing Carter until Saturday afternoon."

"I am so looking forward to this." Zara said.

CHAPTER NINE

Friday night came and as I opened the door to Zara, she said "So this is your little castle?"

"Yes," I said, "what do you think of it?"

"It is absolutely beautiful and the scenery is like a picture postcard. Now I can see why you wouldn't want to come and live in the city."

"Did you pack your pjs?" I asked.

"Of course I did, but I must be off around 10am in the morning , I have lots to do and besides Connor and I are going out."

After dinner, we got into our pyjamas and made ourselves comfy in front of the fire, chatting about everything. "I am really glad you come to work at the office, Anna." Said Zara.

"Me too, we are like little happy family." I replied with a giggle. "And little did I know, it would be there where I would find My King!"

Zara just sat, listening to me talk about my life in the country and also my dreams and wishes for the future. "What a beautiful story, Anna, and to be serious, I think your fairytale has already begun."

"I never in a million years thought I would meet someone like Carter though."

"But Anna, you are very pretty, with long, blonde hair and those big blue eyes...how could he resist? I hope Connor and I can be as in love as you and Carter are. Do you think you will live in the country with Carter, when you get married?" Zara asked.

"Zara, I would truly love that, but I have to wait until he asks me to marry him first!"

"Well, I am nearly sure that's why he is taking you

to Paris." Zara replied.

"Time will tell, Zara." I said.

Shortly after 9.30am the following morning, Zara set off home. "Enjoy tonight!" I called after her, as she replied "And you enjoy Paris, make sure to tell me all about it!"

Saturday evening came and Carter and I talked about Paris. The immense excitement was building up inside me. We spent Saturday night in the cottage and on Sunday morning, he left early for work. Placing a kiss on my head he said "See you on Wednesday, My Queen."

CHAPTER TEN

Wednesday morning finally came. Sitting in the airport, I heard our flight being called. I squeezed Carter's hand in excitement and he looked at me and smiled. "Anna, My queen," he said "this is just one of your dreams, I promise to fulfil the rest."

"We will be arriving in Paris in twenty minutes" I hear the captain announce on the flight. Carter had drifted off into a sleep, I didn't want to wake him. He looked so peaceful, but yet so very tired. I placed my hand on his knee and said "I love you Carter."
And in a clear, silent voice, with his eyes still closed, he replied "Anna, you are the love of my life."

Carter hired a car when we got to Paris. "Now we have got a car, we won't have to worry about transport." Our hotel was beautiful and the moment we entered, I could feel the love and peace the place held. Carter started unpacking our cases and as I sat upon the bed, I watched him hang our clothes, so very neatly on hangers and place them in the wardrobe.
"Tonight, my darling," he said "we shall have dinner here at the hotel and rest, and come tomorrow we shall go and see some of the beautiful sights."
I walked towards Carter, put my arms around his waist and pulled him close to me. As he kissed me passionately, I felt I wanted to ask him to marry me! Now I had to pull myself together, it was up to

Carter to ask, not me. We left our hotel room and went downstairs to have dinner. As we were sitting in the hotel restaurant, I heard the sound of violins. I then noticed three gentlemen standing beside a table, where a young man and women were seated. They were playing the theme music of "Love Story." The girl looked slightly embarrassed, but ever so happy.

"How beautiful and romantic." I said to Carter.

I then watched the man get down on one knee. "Oh my goodness, he has just proposed to her" I said in awe. I felt overjoyed for the girl. She has truly got her dream. Carter took my hand and smiled, "They look so very happy, don't they Anna?" He said.

After the excitement calmed down and we had our meal, we discussed where we shall go first tomorrow. "Oh, I can't wait to see the Eiffel Tower" I said. "Yes, we will see such beauty while we are here." Carter exclaimed.

Am I dropping too many hints?" I asked myself. The Eiffel tower is where I would love Carter to propose to me...that's if he was going to.

We made love several times that night. I still couldn't believe I was here, in Paris, making love to My King. It was heavenly. I always felt safe, laying in Carter's strong arms and listening to the sound of his heartbeat, it made me drift off into a peaceful sleep. A soft tear fell from my eye upon Carter's chest. "Why are you crying Anna?" Carter asked.

"Darling, I am just so happy and I want you to promise me you will never leave me." I replied.

"That, I can promise you, My Queen."

"Why don't we get some sleep now," Carter said

"we will have such a busy day tomorrow" his voice trailed off.

CHAPTER ELEVEN

Driving through Paris and taking in its sights was beautiful. "Everything is so romantic here Carter." I said. *"Yet again dropping more hints..."* I thought to myself.

"If Penny could only see us now... Did I tell you Penny was thinking of buying Mr. Watson's house? "Yes," Carter said "you did."

"I hope she does," I said "it would be just like old times. Maybe I should give her a call before we leave for home and ask her did she go and see Johnathon, Mr. Watson's son. The property has been vacant since his father passed away, and I'm sure if he was to sell it, he would be happy that Penny was the new owner.

Our time in Paris was heavenly. I just didn't want it to end. I can truly say I feel I have the world in my hands when I held Carter. Thinking back to the very first moment, I knew I wanted him.

We drove back to the hotel to shower and have dinner. "Tomorrow night, we shall go to the tower," Carter said, "it seems even more romantic at night time." "Everything is romantic, Carter" I said "the music, the food and the sights are truly wonderful."

The next day we finally arrived at the Eiffel Tower. "This, My Queen is what you have been waiting to see." Carter said. Taking a deep breath, I smiled and said "Yes and it is very breathtaking, isn't it? It is just another part of my dream." "Everything does look so different at night" I said. Overlooking the beauty of Paris at night was truly wonderful.

We had dinner at a beautiful restaurant before returning back to the hotel. I felt slightly disappointed Carter hadn't proposed to me, but I had to keep telling myself it *"just isn't the right time and whatever will be, will be."*

I took Carter's hand and said "thank you darling, I can't put into words how you have made me feel, I must say I feel like the happiest girl in the world."

I gave Penny a quick call later that evening. "Penny, you have no idea how wonderful it is here, in Paris, but when I get home, I shall tell you all about it."

"Anna," Penny said, "I am buying Mr. Watson's house! I saw his son yesterday and he said he was very happy I was the one who was going to buy the house." I was overwhelmed by the news, and I knew as soon as I was home, Penny would be the first person down to my cottage.

"She sounds very happy," I said to Carter as I came off the phone "she's moving back to the country.

We spent our last day in Paris doing some shopping. I wanted to get some souvenirs for Penny and Zara. I knew both girls would be waiting to see my ring, but sadly, they will be disappointed. It was now time to catch our flight home and I couldn't wait to hear all of Penny's good news regarding her new home. Taking one last look around before boarding our flight back to Belfast, I felt very sad. However, I had to be realistic and say to myself *"not everyone goes to Paris just to be proposed to."*

Carter and I had a fabulous time and that meant the world to me. Making myself comfortable in my seat in the plane, I placed my hand against Carter's arm, I was tired and felt myself drifting off to sleep. I felt Carter's hand stroke my cheek as he quietly said "would you like something to drink, My Queen?"

Rubbing my eyes, I said "thank you darling, just some water would be nice" as I drifted off again.

It was raining when we arrived in Belfast. Carter had left his car at the airport so once we got our luggage off, we went to my cottage. "I will just have a quick coffee, Anna, I want to go straight home and let my father know we are back." Said Carter. "I will call you tomorrow, I want you to get a good sleep." He added. "Okay my darling," I said. "safe home and we will talk tomorrow, thank you again for such an amazing time!"

CHAPTER TWELVE

"Hi Penny!" I said as I answered the phone. "How did you know that was me?" she giggled. "I wasn't sure if you were home yet but I've got you anyway, well... tell me all then?"

"Come and see me tomorrow, Penny, I'm really tired and I just want to have an early night." I said.

"Okay then, I shall see you around 10.30am, would that be alright?" Penny said.

"Yes, see you then." I replied.

Before I even had my eyes open the next morning, I could hear Penny knocking the door. "Welcome home!" she squealed as I stood there, still half asleep. "I will make breakfast," I said sleepily, "you go and set the table."

"Well, have you set a date then?" Penny asked.

"A date? Date for what, Penny?" I said.

"You mean Carter didn't ask you to be Mrs. Mcallister?!"

"No, he didn't..." I said, somewhat glum.

"Well, I don't believe it." Penny said in such a serious voice, I had to laugh.

"We had such a fabulous time and to be honest, the time just wasn't right." I said.

"So you are buying Mr. Watson's property?" I asked.

"Yes, everything is going well and I hope to be moving in come December." Penny said enthusiastically.

"Lovely, Penny, I am so happy for you and I am so glad you decided to move back to the country again."

CHAPTER THIRTEEN

The weeks seemed to pass very quickly and everyone at work was talking about Christmas. Zara always decorated the office beautifully and played Christmas music. "This is going to be a very special Christmas" Zara said, "Connor and I shall be spending it together. My parents have invited him to stay at our home all over the Christmas season."

"I am so happy for you, Zara" I said "and you both look amazingly happy together." Zara was planning an evening out on New Year's Eve, but Carter and I will be going down South.

"I'm afraid I won't be able to go" I said to Zara.

"Oh, never worry Anna, you just go and make sure you both have a good time."

Penny was busy adding the finishing touches to her new home, "I'm so glad I am back home, Anna." Penny said.

"So am I, it's just like old times." I said, smiling.

"I would like to go to the auction" Penny said, "and I would love you to come with me."

"Yes, it's on Wednesday night isn't it? I asked.

To which Penny replied "Yes it is."

As we walked around the auction room, I saw Penny's eyes staring at the most beautiful grandfather clock. "Isn't it beautiful?" I said.

"It sure is, Anna." She said, barely taking her eyes off the clock.

"Well then, it's yours." I said.

"Are you serious? I would love it but..."

"But nothing" I said, "It shall be a gift from Carter

and I." I said.

"Oh Anna, you have no idea how much this means to me!" Penny said, overwhelmed.

I went across the room to talk to the auctioneer and within minutes I had bought the clock. "The clock will be delivered to your new house on Friday evening around 7pm" I said to Penny.

I couldn't wait to take Carter to see Penny's new house this weekend. On Friday morning, Carter called me to say he had booked us a hotel for New Year's Eve and he would discuss all the details when he arrived at the cottage later that night. Penny and I had talked about going to New York, but with Penny moving back to the country and Carter and I being in Paris, we decided not to go. Everything always looked so amazing in the country and when the snow fell, it was just like a fairytale. Many times when I was down at the lighthouse, I would look up and see my little cottage, sitting so beautifully at the top of the mountain.

"This is my castle" I said to myself *"and one day I hope my King comes to love it as much as I do."*

Carter decided that we should go and have an overnight at the hotel down South to see what I thought of it, "after all Anna, we will be spending New Year's eve there." Carter said.

"I would love that, and yes, New Year's Eve sounds great." I replied happily.

We set off on our journey down South early on Saturday morning, "wait until you see the hotel, Anna" Carter said "when I saw it, I just had to book us a room for New Year's Eve, it is absolutely amazing and I know you will love it."

"My goodness, look at that castle, Carter" I said "isn't it beautiful?"

"Anna, My Queen that isn't a castle, that is the hotel where you and I are staying!" Carter said, amused.

"You are joking?" I replied.

"No I am not , I told you it was amazing, didn't I? My Queen, I want only the best for you and the best you shall have." Carter said.

I stood in amazement as Carter was checking in, my eyes were nearly popping out of my head as I looked around the place! I had never saw anything like it. Then I noticed the poster on the wall that advertised the New Year's Eve grand ball.

"Oh my goodness, I am going to a ball!" I thought to myself.

Carter opened the door to our room "After you." He said.

"I really can't believe this" I said, this is like something you would see in a fairytale, Carter how did you know about this place?"

"One of the guys at work told me about it and I just couldn't resist." He answered.

My eyes filled up with tears as I said "Oh darling, you really spoil me, don't you?"

"I am a man who is crazy in love and for you My Queen, I shall give whatever your heart desires." Carter said, as my heart melted away.

"This must have cost a fortune, I can't let you pay for all of this, Carter." I said.

As I opened the doors that led out to the balcony, there was a beautifully laid table. It was just outstanding and the scenery overlooking Ireland was astonishing.

"Tonight, My Queen, we shall eat out here. I have already ordered room service for around 8pm." Carter informed me.

"*Wow...*" I thought to myself.

"Let's go and look around the hotel, I want to see every part of this wonderful place. Are you and I going to be attending the New Year's ball?" I inquired.

"Of course we are, that's what I wanted you to see, I thought you would be happy with that?" he smirked.

"Happy? I am bursting with excitement."

Just looking at the marvellous staircase, I pictured myself standing at the top, in my ball gown. "*If only Penny could see this place.*" I thought.

To me, this was a fairytale, but a true one!

"Can I be of any assistance?" I heard a lovely voice ask.

"We are staying here tonight," I said "we will be coming to the ball."

"My name is Molly and I hope you enjoy your stay." The lovely voice replied. Molly was very pleasant and gave Carter and I a tour of the hotel.

"Now then, would you and your husband like to see the ball room?" Molly asked.

I looked at Carter and smiled, "*Husband...*" I said.

We entered the fancy doors of the ball room and Molly turned the lights on so we could see its beauty properly.

"What a room," I said to Molly "I have never seen anything like it!"

Remembering back to my childhood, I saw things like this in my princess books but now, as I was standing in the centre of the room, I thought to myself *"Fairytales do come true then!"*

The stage was at the top of the hall, this is where the band plays. As Molly turned the bright lights on to light up the stage, Carter watched as I walked around the room a few times. The dance floor was very big and there were tables and chairs around the room. The chairs were decorated in white cotton and had a massive green bow around the back rest of them. A beautiful big Christmas tree sat in the corner of the stage, decorated so beautifully.

"It looks so much prettier on New Year's Eve." Molly said, clearly catching me staring.

We made our way out to the garden, where there was a water fountain.

"You can make a wish in the fountain, Anna." Molly said "We have a photographer who would be happy to take some pictures, if you want?"

"Molly, may I ask do you have a hairdresser here?" I asked Molly.

"I would be happy to do your hair, Anna. I don't start work until 7.30pm on the evening of the ball and if you need me, I will come to your room around 6.30pm?"

"That would be wonderful," I said, "I would be so grateful if you could do that for me."

After a romantic dinner out on the balcony, Carter and I made love.

"The touch of your skin drives me insane, Anna. When we make love I feel like I am in paradise" Carter whispered in my ear. The pleasure was overpowering, laying naked in the big bed, and our bodies as one. I was screaming, as Carter said "how could I ever resist you, Anna? I am crazy about you."

Our love making was electric. Our bodies were trembling with desire. As he caressed my breasts, I cried out with pleasure. Finally, we reached that heavenly peak, and looking into each other's eyes, I saw my future with Carter, my true King.

"Oh Penny!" I said as I picked up the telephone to answer the call. "You won't believe it, Carter and I are going to a ball on New Year's Eve. That's why he took me to stay overnight at the hotel. The place is like a castle" I had to catch my breath I was so excited.
"You are a lucky girl, Anna."
"Please come and help me pick my gown?" I asked Penny. "I want to look like a fairytale Queen."
"It would be my pleasure. We should go next Saturday, I am so excited for you" Penny replied.

CHAPTER FOURTEEN

Madison arrived into the office on Monday morning.

"Hi Anna," he said, "you look extremely happy, as usual. How is Carter keeping?"

"Carter is doing just fine, we are going to a ball on New Year's Eve down South." I replied.

"Oh, that sounds lovely, Anna." Madison said.

"So, Zara is still very much in love with Connor" Madison laughed "I have lost two of my delivery guys to you two girls, I do hope Joe doesn't start any more females. Oh well, at least you are two beautiful girls and I wish you both every happiness with Carter and Connor."

Penny and I went to do some Christmas shopping and also get my gown for the ball.

"I know the perfect place in the city where you could get a gown." Penny said.

"I don't care how much it's going to cost, I want the best and most of all, the prettiest." I replied, excitedly.

As we walked into the store, I looked around and saw some beautiful gowns.

"Let me help you." The lady said.

"Hello, my friend is looking for a unique gown. She is going to a ball down South but wants to look like a Queen." Penny said in a funny voice.

"Well you have come to the right place then." The lady said as she shook hands with Penny and I. "I am Rose and I can assure you I have the perfect ball gown for you, Anna!"

Rose let me try on several gowns before she brought that special one from the other room.

"No matter what you try on Anna, they are all extremely beautiful." Penny said as Rose agreed.

When Rose came into the dressing room with this gown, my eyes lit up. "Penny." I said, "Look, isn't it the most beautiful colour?"

The gown was a perfect fit, it was sky blue.

"It goes with the colour of your eye, Anna" Rose stated.

I couldn't take my eyes off the reflection of myself in the mirror.

"And with your long blonde hair, I have the perfect tiara for you." Rose said, happily.

"Oh, Anna." Penny said, "You are going to blow Carter's mind when he sees you."

The tiara was very delicate, with little tiny hearts which had blue diamonds.

"All I need is my glass slipper!" I said to Rose.

"Anna, you have already got your lover's heart." Rose said.

"How do you know that?" I asked.

"Time will tell Anna, just you wait and see."

"You are amazing, Rose and I think I have just found myself a new friend. I shall call in and pick the outfit up a few days before we set off down South, see you soon!" I said.

"Make sure you take lots of pictures and call in and have a chat with me in the new year" Rose said as Penny and I left.

"Rose must know something I don't." I said to Penny.

"Don't be silly, Anna, she was just being polite, she was a lovely lady." Penny replied.

Penny and I stayed in the city most of the day, I felt tiny snowflakes fall.

"I'm cold, Anna. Lets' go and get something to eat. Why don't we put the bags in the car and go to a Chinese restaurant?" Penny said.

"It sure looks and feels like Christmas now!" I heard a man say as he came into the restaurant. The gentleman was covered in snow. "My goodness," Penny said as she looked out the window "It seems we will be having a white Christmas after all."

As we finished our meal, Penny said "Let's start to make our way home, I hope the snow isn't too deep up on the mountain."

Thankfully we got home safe, I had to call Carter to tell him I got my gown and ask him if he got his tuxedo organised.

"Hi, darling" I said as Carter picked up the phone "how was your day?" I asked.

"My day was good, the weather is so very cold but I am glad you got home safe."

"Carter, if the snow continues, will we still be able to travel down South for the New Year?" I asked.

"My Queen, we shall be going even if I have to carry you." Carter said so seriously as I laughed at him.

As I was leaving work on Christmas Eve, I wished all my work colleagues a happy Christmas – "I shall see you all in the new year!" I said.

I gave Zara a big hug and said "I hope you and Connor have a beautiful Christmas together!"

"I am going to miss you Anna." Zara said.

"Now don't you start crying, it's Christmas, and

you and Connor are going to spend your first Christmas together!" I replied, laughing.

When I arrived home, shortly after 5pm, Carter was already at the cottage.

"Hi, Anna, I was starting to get worried about you." He said in his sexy voice.

"Sorry, darling," I said "I just stopped off to get a few bits and pieces, no need to worry now! The next ten days we shall be alone to enjoy." I said.

Everything seems just perfect, Carter and I had decorated the tree and it looked beautiful.

"I am a big child at heart, Anna and when we have children I..." Carter trailed off and went silent. I looked at Carter, he was blushing. He said "Sorry, I guess I am just getting carried away, darling.

To which I replied "I promise you if we are ever blessed with children, you will certainly have your hands full!" I laughed.

Carter and I went to see Penny and take some Christmas presents to her house. We walked up the lane that led us to Penny's house, "this sure brings a lot of memories" I said as I stopped and looked around. It was just like yesterday when Penny and I would talk about our future dreams and wishes. "We had so many years of happiness here." I said to Carter.

"You both will have so many more, don't worry!" Carter replied reassuringly.

Penny looked so extremely happy in her new home and as I watched her buzzing about, I looked at her and said "Penny, welcome home."

On our way back to the cottage, Carter and I couldn't resist having a snowball fight. "We are like two children." I squealed as I tried to run and duck from snowballs Carter was chucking at me.

"Look at that beautiful moon, Anna, isn't it just amazing" Carter said. I stopped to look and at that moment, Carter grabbed me and rolled me in the snow. "Now I have got you!" He said, giggling like a child. We rolled about, giggling, then Carter held me tightly and looked into my eye. His lips met mine and the urge of wanting to make love to him at that moment was driving me insane. "I don't want My Queen to catch a cold," Carter moaned into my ear as he put his hand up my jumper and caressed my breasts while kissing my neck.

"Make love to me now," I sighed "please, Carter!"

It was a beautiful evening as the moon lit up the sky. As we made love we didn't even care or feel the cold. All that mattered was we wanted each other so much, we just couldn't keep our hands off one another. Every time Carter touched me, he drove me wild. Looking into his big, brown eyes and seeing the love he had for me, made me weak. Carter was the most handsome man I had ever set my eyes upon. "You belong to me, Carter." I said.

"I am truly in love with you, Anna and I know I am living every man's dream." He said as we both got up, out of the snow. "Let's make our way back to the cottage, my darling, its staring to snow again."

"I'm going to have a nice, hot bath." I said.

"I'll go check the oven and make sure the turkey hasn't been overcooked, while you, My Queen, have your bath."

CHAPTER FIFTEEN

Carter and I had a wonderful Christmas. I couldn't believe it was only days away that we would be setting off to the beautiful hotel down South again to celebrate the new year.

"I have to go and collect my gown, Darling, but Penny is coming with me. Do you need me to get you anything while I am in the city?" I said.

"No, Anna I will be going to get a few things myself and besides, I arranged to meet Madison for lunch and a chat. Please drive carefully." Carter replied.

"Okay, darling and tell Madison I shall see him in the new year when I return to work." I said as I waved goodbye to Carter.

"I am so excited, Penny, I can't wait. Tomorrow morning, Carter and I will be setting off for the South" I said, barely able to control my voice with excitement.

Rose covered my gown with a large cover to make sure Carter couldn't see it. "I want to surprise him!" I said to her.

"Anna go, and trust me, you will have an amazing time. I hope the snow doesn't get any worse." Rose said. "Don't worry, I will be going to the ball, no matter what!" I laughed.

The day eventually arrived. Carter and I got out of bed just before 8am. We tidied up and then checked our weekend bags to make sure we had everything packed. Shortly after breakfast, Carter put our bags into his car. I laid my gown on the back seats so it didn't get wrinkled. Penny called in for a few minutes before we set off on our journey to Ireland.

"Make sure you guys have a fantastic time and make sure to take plenty of photographs." She said.

We arrived at the hotel at 3pm and as we were checking in, Molly greeted me with a big, friendly hug. "I thought you didn't start work until 7.30pm?" I asked her.

"I don't, but I wanted to be here when you arrived." She said, kindly.

"You are so sweet, Molly." I said.

"Let me help you to your room." Molly said as she carried my gown and laid it across the big, king size bed. "I won't look at it now, Anna," she said, "I want to wait until you're ready to put it on. I shall see you at 6.30pm." And then the door shut behind her.

"Darling," Carter said, "when Molly arrives to do your hair, I shall go downstairs and have a drink and let you get ready."

Carter had a quick shower and put on his jeans and shirt, "this will do me until it's time to put my suit on." He said. "Are you excited, Anna?" Carter asked me.

"Yes I am, but my tummy is so full of nerves!" I laughed.

Molly arrived to our room, as promised at 6.30pm. Now then, Anna, let me help you get ready, she giggled. Carter had already gone downstairs to have a drink and chat to some of the other folk. After my makeup was completed, I gave Molly my beautiful tiara.

"Oh, Anna." Molly said, "I have never seen

anything so beautiful and delicate and just look at the sparkle of the little diamonds."

Brushing my long blonde hair, then rolling it up into a bun, Molly gently placed the tiara on my head. Standing back and looking at me in amazement, Molly said "you sure do have great taste, Anna!"

I went out onto the balcony as Carter was coming into the room to get ready. I didn't want him to see me so I closed the thick, red velvet curtains as I entered the balcony. I listened to Carter sing, he sounds so very happy. I truly want to spend the rest of my life with this man.

"That's me ready, Anna" Carter said, "I shall see you soon!"

"Yes darling," I replied, "I won't be too long."

Just a few minutes after Carter had went downstairs again, Molly arrived back to the room to help me into my gown. As Molly removed the covering from the gown, she laid it back upon the bed, "I have never seen anything so beautiful, Anna." She said.

I didn't want to look in the mirror until I was completely ready. When I had finally got my gown on, I felt the nerves pulse through my entire body. I felt like a queen. Molly looked at me and said "You look amazing, Anna."

Walking towards the mirror, I stopped. Was this really me? I had to fight back the tears as I didn't want to ruin my makeup. "Molly!" I said "Even if I do say so myself, I look outstanding." "Now then, take a few deep breaths and going to your King, after all you are a queen tonight." Molly said, with her sweet smile.

Making my way towards the door, I turned and looked at Molly, "thank you again..." I said. To which Molly interrupted "Go Anna! He is waiting for you."

I could hear all of the voices as I got closer to the top of the stairs. *"My goodness..."* I thought to myself *"there are so many people here."* I must say, all the ladies looked so beautiful. I stood looking over the banister to see if I could see Carter...there he was. Standing there. Waiting for me. His eyes were fixed firmly upon me as I slowly walked down the grand stairs to meet him, he held out his hand. As I reached the last stair, Carter said "My Queen, you are the most beautiful girl in the world, I am the luckiest man on earth."

Carter looked, as always, so very handsome and I knew at that moment, he was mine forever.

"Oh Carter!" I exclaimed, "I am so nervous."
"Please don't be, Anna." He replied, with that reassuring smile.
I felt everyone was looking at me, and obviously Carter noticed my discomfort as he said "Anna, the other girls here are admiring how beautiful you are."

As we were seated in the large restaurant, I couldn't stop myself looking around. I had never seen anything so magical, to me this was a fairytale. Once again, my mind drifted back to when I was a child, thinking of the times I would have said to my father
"I want my life to be a living fairytale." If only he

could see me now.

I had to fight back the tear, they were tears of happiness.

The meal was absolutely delicious, although I couldn't really eat much because the excitement was just unreal! I couldn't wait to get into the ballroom and hold Carter close to me. I was going off in a daydream about the events which were about to unfold when Carter interrupted me "Are you alright, Anna?" He asked.

"Oh, I am sorry, darling I am just so mesmerized and overwhelmed."

"We will be going into the ballroom very soon, Anna!" Carter said.

To which I relied "Carter I must tell you, I am so very happy and I truly love you."

I excused myself and went into the ladies room to touch up my lipstick and perfume. I could hear the band playing and I was just waiting for us to enter that wonderful room.

Carter led me by the hand into the ballroom. My eyes lit up even more as I stood there, speechless. *"This is like a palace,"* I thought to myself *"something I thought I would only ever see in movies."* The large, crystal chandeliers, the high ceilings and the well, it was a breathtaking sight. I didn't realize how tight I was holding Carter's hand until he said

"Anna, take it easy, you are still very nervous I take it?"

"Sorry, I am just overjoyed." I relied, laughing.

We got chatting to a lot of the other folk there and as ladies do, we were saying how beautiful every woman looked.

"May I have the pleasure of this dance, My Queen?" Carter said in a soft, but sexy voice as he stood up to take my hand.

Our eyes locked as we danced to the beautiful waltz. Everyone was so happy and as I placed a gentle kiss on Carter's lips I said "I never want this night to end!"

Later in the evening, I noticed some photographers. "Why don't we get our picture taken, Carter?" I said.

"Yes My Queen, that would be nice." He replied.

One of the ladies came over to me as I was going to sit down and said "I have been watching you since you came into the ball and may I say, your gown is so unique and such a beautiful colour."

"Thank you!" I replied, flattered by the lovely comment from this lady who I had never met.

"And I hope you and your husband have a memorable night together!" she added.

Carter laughed as I told him what the lady had said. "So, she thought you and I were married?" he said. "Anna, My Queen, one day we shall be as one, that I can promise you!"

"Really Carter? When?" the words escaped my mouth before I even realised what I had actually said.

"One day, Anna we shall go to a place where the grass is always green and the skies are always blue, and there, My Queen, we shall live in our very own castle upon the mountain." Carter replied.

My heart skipped a beat as Carter said those words.

The night was finally coming to a close and as we were having our final dance, I held Carter so tight and close to me. It was fast approaching midnight when Carter said "Let us go out into the garden, Anna where we can bring in the New Year alone?"

In less than five minutes, this year will be over and a new one would begin. We walked, hand in hand towards the fountain that was situated in the corner of the lawn. I then noticed, as Carter looked at his watch "Well My Queen," he said, "it's the countdown!"

The folk inside were all counting down the seconds, Carter held both my hands as the bells started ringing at exactly midnight. The first firework lit up the sky and Carter bent down on both knees and said "Anna, please may I ask you to be my wife?"

I burst into tears, and shouted, uncontrollably "Yes, yes, yes, yes! My darling, I will."

With his hands trembling, he opened a tiny, red, velvet box and removed the most stunning, white gold engagement ring. He gently slipped the ring onto my finger as we both cried and hugged one another with immense joy.

"Happy New Year, Anna, and may the rest of our life together be filled with love." Carter said.

We both decided not to have a long engagement, so we set the date for June the 1st, just five months after our engagement and it was also Carter's birthday. Penny was the first person to know about my good news, I called to see her as we got home from down South.

"I knew he would ask you!" she said, "I just had the

feeling. Five months and I shall be your bridesmaid, I must say, he ain't wasting any time! We must start making wedding plans as soon as possible!" Penny said.

CHAPTER SIXTEEN

My first day back at the office, and everyone was in great form. Zara stood, holding my hand, "look at this ring guys!" she squealed. "This is the most beautiful ring I had ever seen" she gushed. "I hope one day Connor gets me a ring like that!"

Just as the words came out of Zara's mouth, Connor and Madison walked into the office. She blushed, gave a slight cough and said "Hi guys!"

Madison stood, smiling at me and with his arms outstretched, said "come on Anna, give me a hug!"

"So your King eventually asked you then?"

"Yes, he did and to be honest I really didn't expect it. Did you know about this?" I asked Madison.

"Yes, I did, but I promised not to breathe a word to anyone until that ring was on your finger." Carter replied.

"Well...did Carter tell you we wanted to ask you to be best man at our wedding?" I asked.

"Yes, I would be absolutely honoured," he replied, "five months is just around the corner, so you're going to be a busy girl."

"I am so happy, Madison. Since the day I first saw Carter I knew I was in love." I said with a smile.

The weeks were passing by very quickly, the wedding preparations were going just as planned. Finally, in six weeks, I shall be Carter's wife, Penny and Zara were both overjoyed that they were to be my bridesmaids. Madison was also so proud he was our best man. I decided to walk up the aisle alone to stand and take the hand of my King, as my father wasn't here to place my hand in Carter's hand. I didn't want anyone else to do this. I knew my father was never far away from me. Carter and I decided to spend May Day with Zara and Connor, we talked about the wedding and our honeymoon. "I still don't know where we are going!" I laughed.

"Anna, Carter said it's a surprise!" Zara moaned.

"But I need to know! If we are going abroad, I will have to go shopping for new holiday clothes." I said.

Zara had made a picnic and she brought more food than we could eat. As we were sitting at the waterfall, Zara said "Anna, this place is beautiful. I could live in the country myself."

We returned back to the cottage for a coffee before Zara and Connor set off home. Carter decided to go put fuel in the bike and check the tyre pressure as he would be leaving at 6am the following morning for work.

"I shouldn't be gone too long, My Queen." Carter said as he left.

Carter was no sooner gone when I heard the great bang. As I ran outside, I saw Carter's bike laying on its side. Where was Carter? I screamed his name as I ran towards the motorbike.

"HELP!" I yelled at the top of my voice, "Somebody please help me!"

Carter had tried to avoid hitting a fox that scuttled across the road as he was driving down the lane, but he lost control of the bike and hit a stone ballard.

The police and ambulance seemed to arrive in minutes. "Please save my fiance!" I pleaded. "We are getting married in six weeks."

"Anna!" I heard Penny call as she ran down the lane. She burst into tears.

"Please let me see Carter." I said as I tried to push past the policemen.

"Please, madam," the officer said, "let the medical team attend to your partner."

Penny was holding me tightly as the paramedics walked towards us.

"I am so very sorry, Madam, we did everything we could but Carter didn't survive."

"Let me see him!" I screamed.

Penny and a policewoman led me up the lane to the cottage.

"Why did this happen?" I cried as I fell on my knees.

After a service in the little church down in the valley, Carter was laid to rest. I go to his resting place everyday to lay a fresh red rose.

I discovered I was pregnant with Carter's baby, shortly after Carter died. I know when it is time for our baby to be born, Carter will be there, with me, in spirit.

"I will never leave you, Anna." That was always Carter's words to me. Fate changed that.

I felt Carter's presence the night Charlie was born and I know not even in death would he leave me.

14933735R00045

Printed in Great Britain
by Amazon.co.uk, Ltd.,
Marston Gate.